P9-CEL-421

THE
BAREFOOT BOOK OF
ANIMAL
TALES
From Around the World

Barefoot Books
2067 Massachusetts Avenue
Cambridge, MA 02140

Text copyright © 1996 by Naomi Adler
Illustrations copyright © 1996 by Amanda Hall
The moral right of Naomi Adler to be identified as the author and
Amanda Hall to be identified as the illustrator of this work has been asserted

First hardcover edition published in 1996 in the United States of America
by Dial Books as *The Dial Book of Animal Tales*. This paperback edition
first published in the United States of America in 2004 by Barefoot Books, Inc.
All rights reserved. No part of this book may be reproduced in any form or by any means,
electronic or mechanical, including photocopying, recording, or by any information storage
and retrieval system, without permission in writing from the publisher

The art for this book was rendered in watercolor and crayon
The book was typeset in Monotype Imprint 12pt on 22pt leading

Graphic design by designsection, England
Printed in Hong Kong / China by South China Printing Co. (1988) Ltd.

This book is printed on 100% acid-free paper

Library of Congress Cataloging-in-Publication Data

Adler, Naomi.
    The barefoot book of animal tales from around the world / retold by Naomi Adler ;
illustrated by Amanda Hall.
Originally published: London: Barefoot Books Ltd, 1996.
[80] p. : col. ill. ; cm.
Summary: A collection of nine tales about animals from different cultures all over the world.

ISBN 1-84148-547-0

1. Animals—Folklore—Juvenile literature. 2. Tales—Juvenile literature. [1. Animals—
Folklore. 2. Folklore.] I. Hall, Amanda, ill. II. Title.
398.2 21   CIP   PZ8.1.A35   2002

The text for "Grandmother Spider" has been adapted from Alida Gersie and Nancy King's
Storymaking in Education and Therapy, published by Jessica Kinglsley Publishers, London.

1 3 5 7 9 8 6 4 2

THE

BAREFOOT BOOK OF

ANIMAL

TALES

From Around the World

Retold by **NAOMI ADLER**

Illustrated by **AMANDA HALL**

Barefoot Books
Celebrating Art and Story

For my beloved friend Margaret Button – N. A.

For Jean and John – A. H.

CONTENTS

GRANDMOTHER SPIDER

NATIVE AMERICAN/CHEROKEE

Long, long ago there were only animals living on the earth. The lands of the north were covered in darkness. For millions of years the animals were content to live in this darkness. However, there came a time when they realized that they were always bumping into one another; they were always falling down holes in the ground; they were always stumbling as they ran around. There came a time when they decided that something must be done about living in such darkness.

Wise Owl declared, "Let us have a gathering of all the animals in the Northern Lands."

A special place and time were appointed for the meeting. Animals arrived from far and wide, all bringing their ideas and their hopes.

Wise Owl called out, "What should we do, my brothers and sisters? It is always dark here, and times are becoming difficult. We must make changes, but how?"

Old Crow was the first to speak out. "I have heard on my many flights that there are animals on the other side of the world who live in the light."

Great Bear asked, "What is the meaning of *light*?"

Old Crow replied, "Where there is light, animals can see all around them. They can see the whole countryside. They can even see each other."

The animals of the dark place became very excited by Old

Crow's words. They all said, "We must have this light, so that we too can see where we are going."

Old Crow continued, "Maybe the animals of the light place will share some of this light with us?"

Brother Fox called out, "No, no! I am sure they will not want to share the light with us. This light must be very precious. We will have to steal it and bring it back here."

Brother Otter popped his head out of the water and said, "It's all very well, but who will go to the place of light? The journey is long and dangerous."

The bravest and strongest animals began to argue. They all insisted that they were the fastest, or the most cunning, or the most clever. At last Brother Possum spoke up above all the noise and quarreling. "I will go, my brothers, because I can hide the light under my bushy tail and so bring it to our dark space."

Finally all the animals agreed that Brother Possum should be the one to go. And so Brother Possum set out on his long journey to the land of light on the other side of the world.

The journey was full of dangers and difficulties, but Brother Possum was very determined and very curious. On and on he traveled. As he came closer to the place of light, his eyes began to hurt — he had not expected such brightness! He squinted his eyes very hard to protect them. Even today if you look closely at a possum, you will see his eyes are almost closed.

At last Brother Possum arrived at the center of the light. He carefully took a piece of light and placed it under his bushy tail. Then he started his journey home. But the light under his tail was so hot, so fierce, that it burned all the bushy fur off his tail, leaving nothing but skin and bone. Even today if you look closely at a possum's tail, you will find it is nothing but skin and bone.

By the time Brother Possum arrived back at the Northern Lands, the light had all vanished. The animals were waiting for Brother Possum. The animals were waiting for the light. How very disappointed they were when he returned empty-handed.

Brother Buzzard spoke out, "I will go to the land of light and I will bring some light back." Brother Buzzard flew high into the sky so that no one would see him when he arrived at the other side of the world. The flight was long and tiring. Finally he reached the center of the light space. Brother Buzzard hovered around the light and dove down with such speed, he was able to take a little bit of light and place it on top of his head. Then he started his long flight home.

The light balancing on top of his head was so hot, so fierce, that it burned a bald patch. Even today if you look closely at a buzzard, you will see a bald patch on his head.

By the time Brother Buzzard arrived back in the dark land, the light had vanished. The animals were waiting for Brother Buzzard. The animals were waiting for the light. How very disappointed they were when he returned empty-handed.

The animals were very sad. They cried out, "Our strongest and bravest brothers have tried and have failed to bring us some light. We are still in darkness!"

Suddenly they heard a tiny, creaky voice. "Excuse me, brothers. You have tried your best. Now it is time for your sister to go and get the light."

The animals looked all around them, trying to discover who the speaker was. But, of course, they could not see anyone. "Who is speaking?" they called out.

"It is I, Grandmother Spider," she answered. "I am very old and very small, but I have a good plan. I would like to try to bring back the light from the other side of the world."

The animals were sure that Grandmother Spider could not possibly succeed, but they agreed to give her a chance and let her go.

Grandmother Spider scuttled to a place deep in the earth that was rich with clay. She took a little piece of clay and molded it into a small pot, with a lid that fit perfectly. She then took the pot, holding it with one of her eight legs, and she started her long journey to the other side of the world, to the place of light. All the while she was spinning her web, leaving a trail behind her, so that she would find her way home.

Grandmother Spider arrived at the center of the light. She took a small piece of light and put it into her pot. She secured the lid tightly, so that the light would not escape. She started her long journey home, following the web trail she had left behind. Even today if you look carefully at a spider's web, you will see that it is just like the rays of the sun.

The animals were waiting for Grandmother Spider. The animals were waiting for the light. As soon as she arrived back in the land of darkness, Grandmother Spider asked the animals to form a circle all around her. Then she lifted the lid of her pot, and there was light all over the place of darkness. It was of such radiance, such splendor, that the animals were amazed. From then on, there was day and there was night in the Northern Lands.

The animals were overjoyed. They could at last see where they were going. They had a great celebration, with singing and dancing, in honor of Grandmother Spider. As for Grandmother Spider, she retreated quietly into the forest, climbed a tall tree, and began to spin a web.

Even today if you look very carefully, you will see that she is still spinning.

THE RABBIT IN THE MOON

INDIAN

Have you ever looked up at the moon when she is full and bright? Have you ever wondered what that silver blue shape is on the moon's surface? This shape, if you look carefully, has the long ears and the body of a rabbit — even the little bobtail is there.

The next time there is a full moon, take the chance to look deeply and silently and then you may very well see this most delightful of animals looking back at you.

You may ask, how did the rabbit get up there? And why is it a rabbit when there are so many other animals to choose from?

Once I met an old Indian storyteller, and she told me how it was that the rabbit ended up on the moon. . . .

14

A very long time ago in a land
called India, there was the most beautiful
forest that you could ever imagine. There were
trees of every shape, size, and shade of green.
There were magnificent flowers on the forest
floor, letting off sweet, sweet smells. The trees were
laden with every kind of fruit and blossom. Birds and
beasts lived in that forest for thousands and thousands
of years.

Among all the animals that lived in this enchanted forest, there
were four who became the best of friends. They were the monkey,
the otter, the elephant, and the rabbit. These four animals loved
each other dearly. But most of all they loved the rabbit. In fact, all
the animals of the forest loved the rabbit more than
anyone else in the world. You see, the rabbit was a
very special being. She was wise and fearless.
She was generous and pure. But most of all she had
a heart of gold. Very often you could see the rabbit
sitting in the middle of the glade surrounded by all the animals of
the forest. She would tell them wondrous stories; she would tell
them of the power that plants and flowers have to heal and
restore. She would tell them of the power that love and kindness
have to transform. She would tell them of the stars and the planets
and of the energies and the magic that is all around. Even the

most fierce of all the animals would come to such gatherings. The tiger came and so did the crocodile. The wolf came and so did the vulture. The rabbit didn't just speak of beautiful things and glorious powers, but she lived them too. Her kindness and gentleness shone from within her like the light shines from the moon. And all who came close to her were inspired by her presence.

And so it was that her three closest friends began to change. The monkey, who had always been naughty and mischievous, planning tricks and teasing everyone, now became more considerate and helpful to others. The otter, who had always been greedy and kept all the fish for himself, now began to share and became helpful to others. The elephant, who had always been secretive, never telling the other animals where the springs and water holes were, now began to share her knowledge and became helpful to others. And as for the rabbit, she also became even kinder, and the glow of

kindness from her heart shone even brighter than before.

One day the rabbit had a brilliant idea. She called her friends. "I have a suggestion to make. We have so much food and water between us. We have so much love and friendship between us. Why don't we offer our skills and our food to the world around us? There are so many beggars and so many hungry children. Let's offer them a little of ourselves."

At the very instant the rabbit was speaking, the great heavenly spirit was passing by and heard every word she said. He could hardly believe his own ears, so he decided to pay great attention to what would happen next.

The rabbit continued, "Look, my friends. Look at the moon dressed in all her radiance, shining silver rays across the darkness of night. With her light she transforms the darkness into clarity and brightness. We could do the same with the power of our love and kindness. We could transform sadness and hardship. Let us bring happiness to whomever enters the forest tomorrow."

The others agreed that this was a splendid idea. That night, sitting under a tree covered with red blossoms in the light of the full moon, the four animals made plans for the next day.

The otter made a vow to catch fish and give all his fish away. The monkey made a vow to pick ripe mangoes and give all his mangoes away. The elephant made a vow to find a new spring and give the water away. And so they fell fast asleep. But the rabbit simply couldn't get to sleep at all because she was thinking and thinking about what she could give. "My only food is green grass, which most creatures do not enjoy. I have nothing at all to give a stranger." All night long she gazed up at the full moon. Just before her eyes finally closed, a terrible thought came to her. She remembered that humans love to eat the flesh of a rabbit. She took a deep breath and made a vow to give herself away. A great feeling of warmth and joy came over her, and the little rabbit fell asleep too.

The heavenly being was listening all the time and he heard this amazing vow. He decided to come down to earth disguised as a beggar and put the rabbit to the test. It was so remarkable that a mere rabbit would offer such a wondrous and unselfish thing.

The next day while the creatures of the forest were all resting under the shade of the leafy trees, they heard a voice calling out in the distance. "Help me, please help me. I'm lost in the forest. I'm hungry and I'm thirsty."

Hearing these cries, the animals ran toward the beggar.

"Don't worry, dear man," they said. "We will take care of you, we will feed you, we will bring you water, and we will help you find your way."

The monkey instantly jumped to a mango tree and brought down an armful of big red juicy mangoes. He placed the mangoes before the beggar.

The otter instantly dove into the river and caught several plump, silver fish and placed the fish before the beggar.

The elephant instantly ran to the new spring and drew out a trunkful of clear, sweet water and brought it to the beggar to drink and to bathe in.

The rabbit instantly placed herself before the beggar and said, "Make a strong fire and I will jump into it so that you can eat of my flesh."

The great spirit in disguise was astonished at this bravery.

He snapped his fingers and made a strange sound with his voice. And there before them was a roaring fire. The rabbit, without thinking another thought, jumped into the blaze. But not a hair of her soft fur was burned, not an inch of her body was scorched, for in that very instant the heavenly being caught the rabbit in the palm of his hand, saying, "Such love and courage are beyond anything I have ever witnessed on earth. This selfless deed must be told to all the world. I shall place you, my little rabbit, in the moon for all to see, for all to learn, for all to remember. You will appear with every full moon, and your power of kindness and love will shine in the silver light of the moon across the whole wide world."

With these words he lifted the rabbit into the sky and placed her on the moon where she still lives to this very day.

So, dear children, the next time the moon is full, go out and look at the night sky and there you will see for yourselves the very rabbit I have told you about. Remember the story, and remember that if you give something precious away, you may receive something back that is very special.

THE DRAGON AND THE COCKEREL

CHINESE

There was once a time when dragons were not yet fully formed and when cockerels had tails like those of peacocks and antlers like those of stags. It was during those ancient times that this story occurred.

The celestial emperor ruled over the sky, the sea, and the earth. Every New Year he held a great celebration up in his heavenly palace in the sky. Important guests from the many different stars and planets were invited, and among them, all the animals of the earth.

The animals of the earth loved going to this yearly event up in the sky and they spent many weeks busily preparing themselves, making themselves as beautiful as could be.

Only Dragon was miserable. He felt himself to be the most dull and boring creature in all China. You see, in those days Dragon had the head of a camel, the eyes of a demon, the neck and body of a snake, the legs of a tiger, and the claws of an eagle. But the fact that he had nothing on top of his head caused him the greatest shame.

One day, as Dragon was swimming in the river, Cockerel came strutting by. Cockerel looked magnificent with his gorgeous tail fanned open and those huge antlers on top of his head. Dragon looked longingly at the antlers.

If only I could have such a splendid headdress, then I wouldn't look so dull anymore, he thought to himself.

Suddenly he had a bright idea. He called out to Cockerel, "Hello there, Cockerel!"

"Good day, Dragon! Why do you look so sad?" asked Cockerel.

Dragon replied, "I am so sad because I have nothing to wear on my head when I go to the New Year celebration. Will you lend me your antlers please, Cockerel?"

Cockerel was amazed. "Certainly not! I am also invited to the party and I need to wear my antlers myself."

Dragon said, "But Cockerel, you look so beautiful with your gorgeous tail. Your antlers only detract from your splendor."

"No, no, Dragon! I need my antlers," shouted Cockerel.

At that moment a very distinguished carp raised her head out of the water. She had heard the entire conversation and since she was rather fond of Dragon she said, "Dragon is quite right, Cockerel. You are indeed more dazzling without your antlers. They do seem to detract from your splendor. Why don't you lend them to Dragon, and I will guarantee their safe return."

In the end, vain Cockerel was persuaded that he was even more beautiful without his antlers. Cockerel agreed, "Alright, I shall lend you my antlers for one day and one night. You must return them as soon as the New Year celebration is over."

Dragon promised that he would.

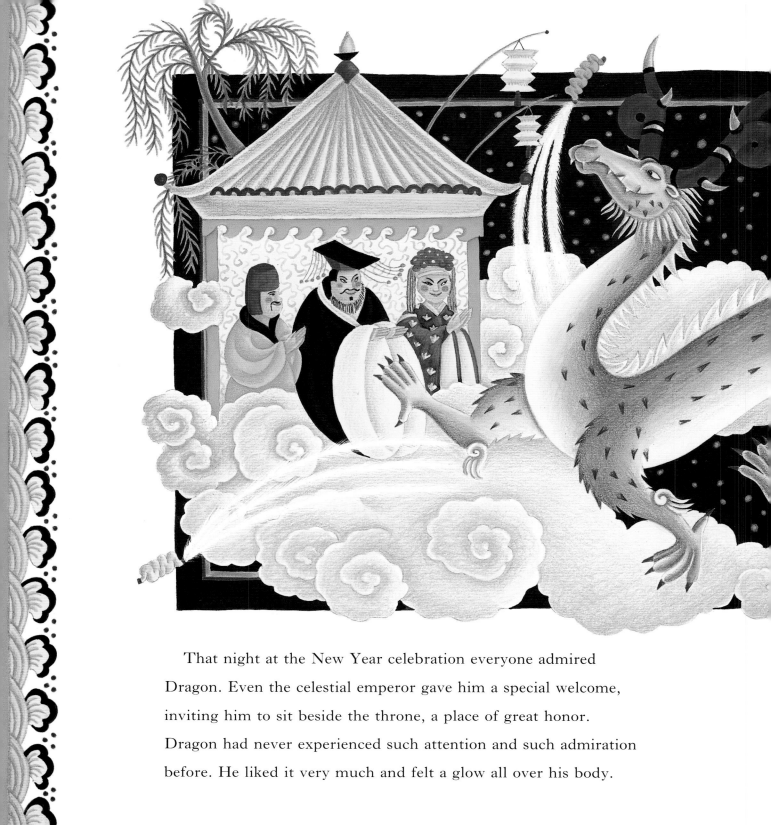

That night at the New Year celebration everyone admired
Dragon. Even the celestial emperor gave him a special welcome,
inviting him to sit beside the throne, a place of great honor.
Dragon had never experienced such attention and such admiration
before. He liked it very much and felt a glow all over his body.

However, Cockerel was extremely jealous when he saw Dragon held in such great esteem and he wished he had kept the antlers for himself. Very early the next morning he rushed over to the river where Dragon lived.

He called out, "Dragon, give me back my antlers!"

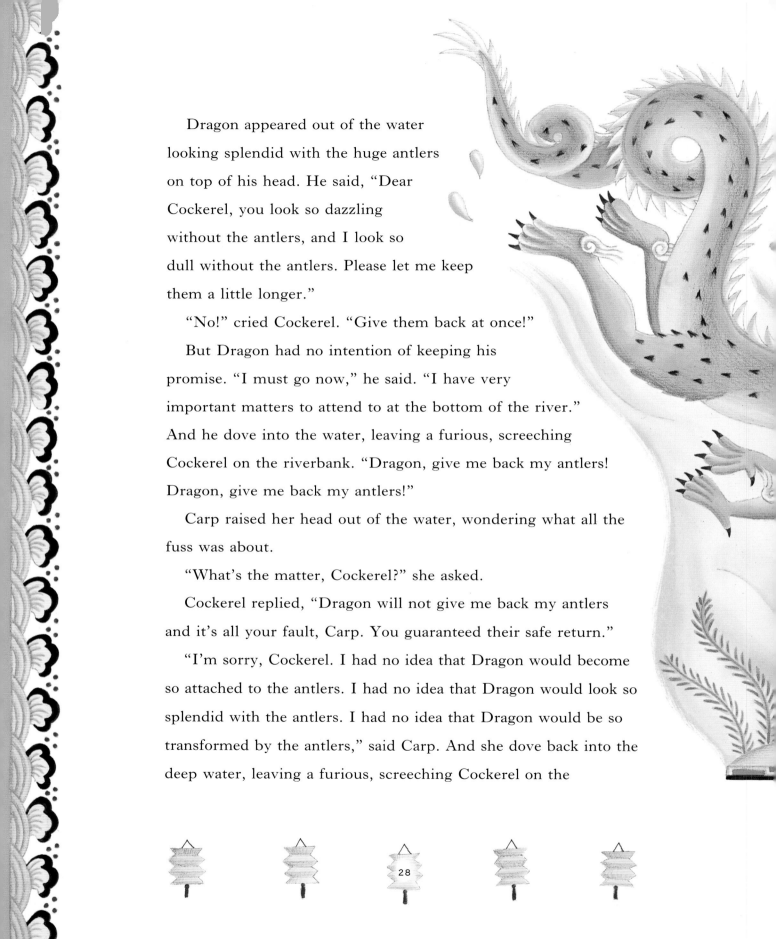

Dragon appeared out of the water looking splendid with the huge antlers on top of his head. He said, "Dear Cockerel, you look so dazzling without the antlers, and I look so dull without the antlers. Please let me keep them a little longer."

"No!" cried Cockerel. "Give them back at once!"

But Dragon had no intention of keeping his promise. "I must go now," he said. "I have very important matters to attend to at the bottom of the river." And he dove into the water, leaving a furious, screeching Cockerel on the riverbank. "Dragon, give me back my antlers! Dragon, give me back my antlers!"

Carp raised her head out of the water, wondering what all the fuss was about.

"What's the matter, Cockerel?" she asked.

Cockerel replied, "Dragon will not give me back my antlers and it's all your fault, Carp. You guaranteed their safe return."

"I'm sorry, Cockerel. I had no idea that Dragon would become so attached to the antlers. I had no idea that Dragon would look so splendid with the antlers. I had no idea that Dragon would be so transformed by the antlers," said Carp. And she dove back into the deep water, leaving a furious, screeching Cockerel on the riverbank, calling out, "Cock-a-doodle-doo! Cock-a-doodle-doo!"

So when you next hear a cockerel calling out at dawn, "Cock-a-doodle-doo! Cock-a-doodle-doo!" you will now know that he is calling out, "Dragon, give me back my antlers! Dragon, give me back my antlers!"

As for the dragon, he became China's most revered creature. The celestial emperor bestowed on him the gift of flight, and the guardianship of all the waters in the sky, sea, and earth.

(The dragon also became the keeper of the magic pearl — but that's another story.) Even today the dragon is invited to celebrate the Chinese New Year and dance the Dance of the Dragon with the people of China.

THE GREEDY FROG

AUSTRALIAN

Before Dreamtime the earth was dead. There were no mountains, no rivers, no animals, no people. It was dark and dry. There was no rain, no wind — only silence and emptiness. Then something began to change. Dreamtime came to be, and wonderful and strange things began to happen. The world was being created. The rainbow serpent came down from the sky and as he slithered across the world, the earth began to move, mountains rose, and valleys appeared. The earth cracked and rivers flowed. Slowly the earth was covered with trees and plants, flowers and herbs. Animals were blown in by the great winds.

In those days when the earth was green and beautiful, there lived a gigantic frog. His name was Tiddalick. Now, this frog was

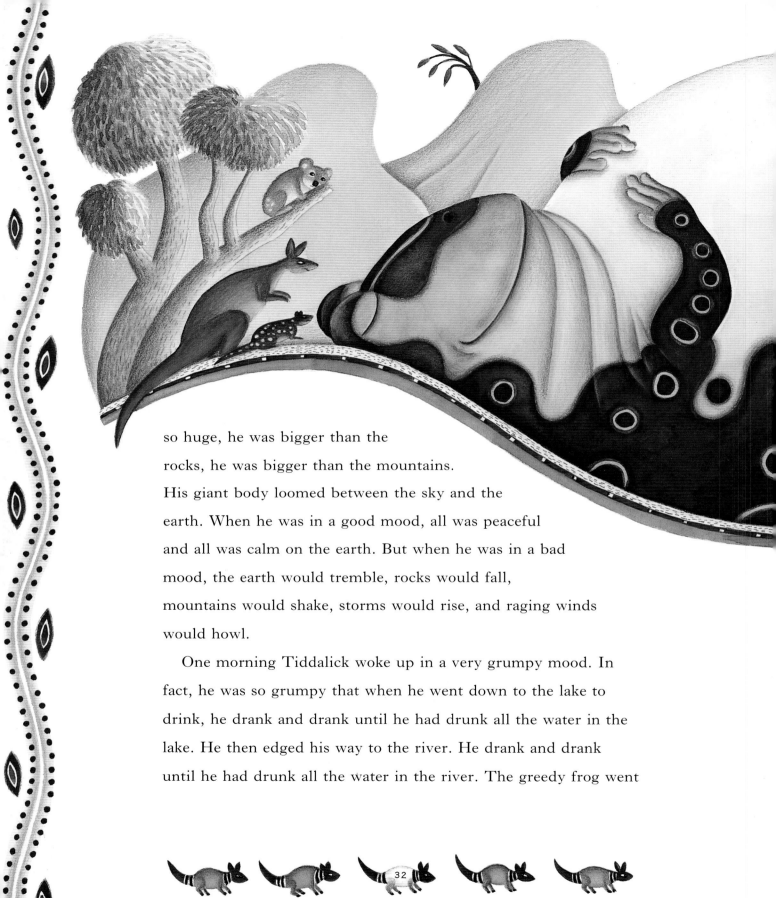

so huge, he was bigger than the
rocks, he was bigger than the mountains.
His giant body loomed between the sky and the
earth. When he was in a good mood, all was peaceful
and all was calm on the earth. But when he was in a bad
mood, the earth would tremble, rocks would fall,
mountains would shake, storms would rise, and raging winds
would howl.

One morning Tiddalick woke up in a very grumpy mood. In
fact, he was so grumpy that when he went down to the lake to
drink, he drank and drank until he had drunk all the water in the
lake. He then edged his way to the river. He drank and drank
until he had drunk all the water in the river. The greedy frog went

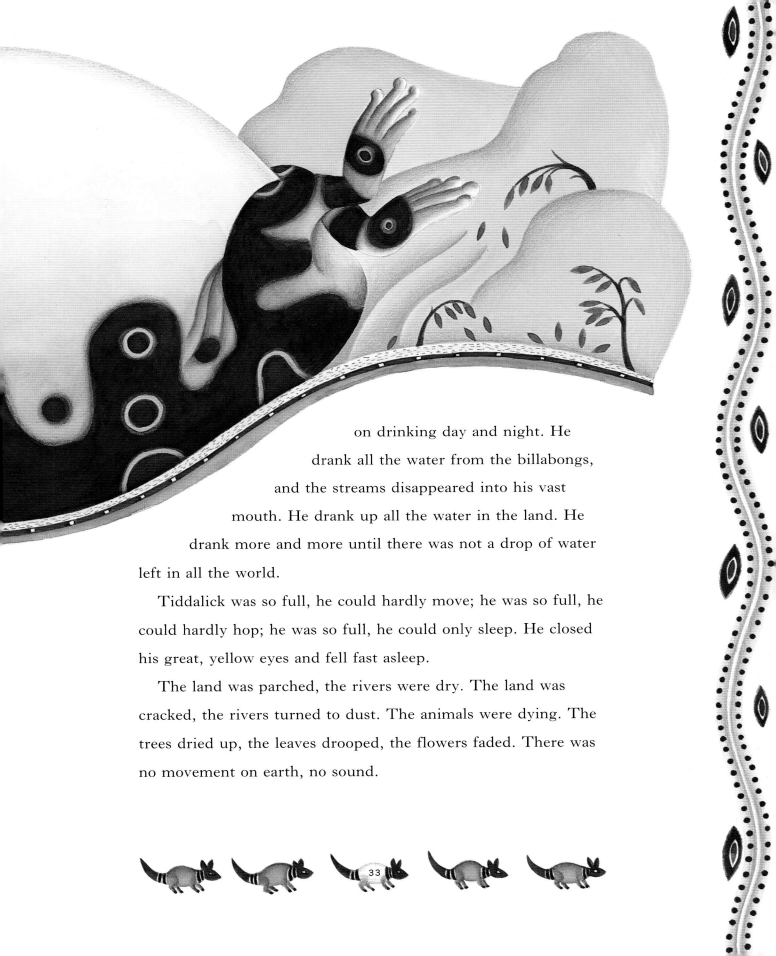

on drinking day and night. He drank all the water from the billabongs, and the streams disappeared into his vast mouth. He drank up all the water in the land. He drank more and more until there was not a drop of water left in all the world.

Tiddalick was so full, he could hardly move; he was so full, he could hardly hop; he was so full, he could only sleep. He closed his great, yellow eyes and fell fast asleep.

The land was parched, the rivers were dry. The land was cracked, the rivers turned to dust. The animals were dying. The trees dried up, the leaves drooped, the flowers faded. There was no movement on earth, no sound.

With their last bit of strength, the animals gathered together in great distress. They cried, "Tiddalick has every drop of water in his belly. We have nothing to drink, we have nothing to eat. There is no rain, there is no water. What should we do?"

The wise old wombat said, "Let us go one by one and plead with Tiddalick to give us back our water." One by one the animals went to Tiddalick. The first one was the kangaroo. She said, "I am the kangaroo, the joyful, jumping kangaroo. But now I have no strength left to jump. All I can do is lie in the dust. Please give us back our water."

Then the dingo came. "I am the dingo who barks and howls in the night. I have no strength left to bark. All I can do is lie in the dust. Please give us back our water."

Then came the kookaburra. "I am the kookaburra. I tell funny stories and jokes. I have no strength left to joke. All I can do is lie in the dust. Please give us back our water."

But it was no good. Tiddalick didn't even open his eyes. It seemed that very soon all the animals would surely die, and the greedy, grumpy frog would be the only one left alive.

The animals thought and thought about a way to solve this

problem. They were just about to give up and lie in the dust and die, when a small voice said, "I have an idea."

They all got up and looked around. There was the little bandicoot flapping his large ears.

He continued, "If we could only make Tiddalick laugh, then all the water from inside him would blow out of his mouth."

So the animals mustered up their very last little bits of strength and made a circle all around the giant frog's resting place. Hundreds and hundreds of animals came, also the birds and insects, to see if any of them could make Tiddalick laugh.

First the kookaburra told his funniest stories. Everyone else laughed and laughed, but Tiddalick didn't. He didn't even open his eyes.

Next the emu and the kangaroo jumped over each other again and again, around and around in the circle. Everyone else laughed and laughed, but Tiddalick didn't. He didn't even open his eyes.

Then lizard came and made the funniest faces, sticking out his tongue and turning around and around on his hind legs. Everyone else laughed and laughed, but Tiddalick didn't. He didn't even open his eyes.

The animals called out, "Come on, Tiddalick, laugh, you big, fat, bloated, squelchy frog. If you could only see yourself, you would laugh until you cried."

It was hopeless. The animals thought that they were doomed and they gave up all hope of ever drinking again.

Just then they heard a strange, tiny cry, "Let me try, let me try." It was Noyang the eel, driven from his favorite creek by the drought. He slithered up to the fat, gloomy frog and began to dance. First his movements were slow and graceful. Soon he danced faster and faster, wriggling and twisting, making himself into the weirdest and funniest shapes. Coiling like a spiral, then jumping up and uncoiling in the air, bouncing and twirling. Then he finished up by jumping onto the frog's fat tummy and whirling and whirling, spinning around and around like Wurrawilberoo the whirlwind.

Tiddalick started to quiver. The quiver got larger and larger until it became a giggle. The giggle got larger and larger until it became a gurgle. The gurgle got larger and larger until the whole earth shook and trembled. All at once he burst out laughing. The animals ran for shelter as the water came gushing out of his mouth like a waterfall tumbling down a mountain.

Tiddalick laughed until every drop of water was out of his belly, flowing away, filling up lakes and ponds, swamps and rivers.

Once again fresh life appeared all over the earth. The whole world woke up as if from a deep sleep. Animals and birds, plants and trees began to move and go about their work as before. Slowly the earth became beautiful again.

However, to this day the Aborigines know that when they see little frogs, descendants of Tiddalick, filling themselves up with water and then burying themselves in the ground, there is going to be a drought.

THE MUSICIANS OF BREMEN

GERMAN

Along time ago there was a farmer who had a donkey that served him faithfully for many long years. While he was able, the donkey carried sacks of grain to the mill and sacks of flour and potatoes to the market. However, as the years passed, the donkey grew old and weak and could no longer serve the farmer as he used to. The farmer planned to send the donkey far, far away for ever and ever. The old donkey heard of this plan and was very sad that this was to be his reward for years of faithful service. The donkey didn't want to go far, far away for ever and ever.

38

So one night as he was standing in the middle of a green field, he looked up at the moon. She was full and glowing. He closed his eyes and said deep, deep inside himself, "I must find a solution. I must find a solution. Please, great moon, shining so brightly, please can you help me to be free?" The very moment that he opened his eyes again, a thought came to him. He knew exactly what he was going to do.

"Of course," he cried. "I will run away. I will run along the road to Bremen to become a musician."

The donkey felt a great wave of warmth inside him. He felt a great strength inside him. He started running across the field, and with all his might he jumped over the fence. He was out! He was free! He trotted along the road to Bremen. He was on a journey toward a new life, a new chance. The old donkey was happy. He set off along the road into the wide world, singing as he went.

On and on he went along the road, until all of a sudden he saw something by the wayside. It was an old dog. A very sad old dog.

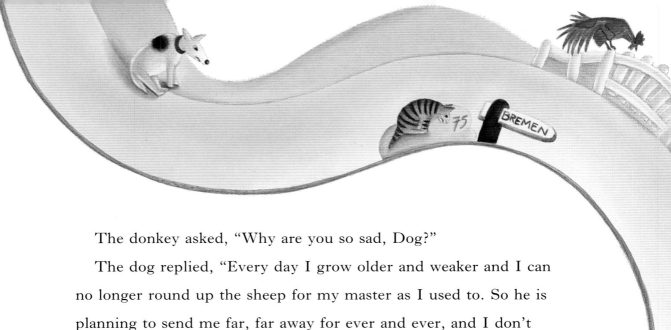

The donkey asked, "Why are you so sad, Dog?"

The dog replied, "Every day I grow older and weaker and I can no longer round up the sheep for my master as I used to. So he is planning to send me far, far away for ever and ever, and I don't want to go far, far away for ever and ever."

"Well!" said the donkey. "Why don't you run away with me to Bremen and become a musician?"

"Yes, please, I'd like that," said the dog, wagging his tail.

So the old donkey, followed by the old dog, set off along the road into the wide world, singing as they went.

On and on they went along the road, until all of a sudden they saw something in the distance. It was a very, very sad old cat sitting on a milestone beside the road.

The donkey asked, "Why are you so sad, Cat?" The cat replied, "Every day I grow older and weaker and I can no longer catch the mice in the house. So my mistress is planning to send me far, far away for ever and ever, and I don't want to go far, far away for ever and ever."

"Well!" said the donkey. "Why don't you run away with us to Bremen and become a musician?"

"Yes, please," said the old cat, jumping onto the road and

stretching her body.

So the old donkey, followed by the old dog, followed by the old cat, set off along the road into the wide world, singing as they went.

On and on they went along the road, until all of a sudden they saw something in the distance. It was a very, very sad old cock perched on top of the farm gate.

The donkey asked, "Why are you so sad, Cock?" The cock replied, "Every day I get older and weaker and I no longer wake up my mistress on time in the morning. So she is planning to send me far, far away for ever and ever, and I don't want to go far, far away for ever and ever."

"Well!" said the donkey. "Why don't you run away with us to Bremen and become a musician?"

"Yes, please," said the cock, flapping his wings and jumping down onto the road.

So the old donkey, followed by the old dog, followed by the old cat, followed by the old cock, set off along the road into the wide world, singing as they went.

41

On and on they went along the road, until they were so tired they could go no farther.

The donkey suggested, "Let's spend the night under this big oak tree." The donkey leaned against the trunk, the dog and the cat lay down in the moss at the foot of the tree, and the cock flew high up and perched on a branch. Before he went to sleep, he looked around the countryside. He saw a little spark of light in the distance. He called out to his companions, "There is a cottage over there, friends, and it's not far away."

The donkey said, "If that is so, we had better get up and go toward it, for it's not very comfortable in this place."

And the dog continued, "Yes, indeed! A couple of bones with meat on them would be very acceptable."

The donkey, the cat, and the cock all agreed that a little hay, fish, and corn would be welcome after such a long journey. So the four friends set out in the direction of the light.

They went on until they reached the cottage. The donkey went right up to the window and looked in.

"What can you see there, Donkey?" asked the inquisitive cock.

"I can see a table spread with food and drink, and around the table are seven robbers," replied the donkey.

"That sounds just right for us," said the dog.

"Yes, yes, I wish we were sitting there," said the donkey.

The cat asked, "But how are we going to get rid of those robbers?"

The donkey turned his head upward and looked at the moon; she was full and glowing bright in the dark sky. He closed his eyes and said deep, deep inside himself, "I must find a solution." The old donkey then opened his eyes and at that very moment it came to him in a flash; he knew exactly what they must all do.

"I have a plan," he said.

The donkey placed his forefeet on the window ledge and called out, "Dog, sit on my back! Cat, sit on Dog's back! Cock, perch on Cat's back, and when I give the signal, we will all make music."

When they were all in position, Donkey gave the signal and the music began.

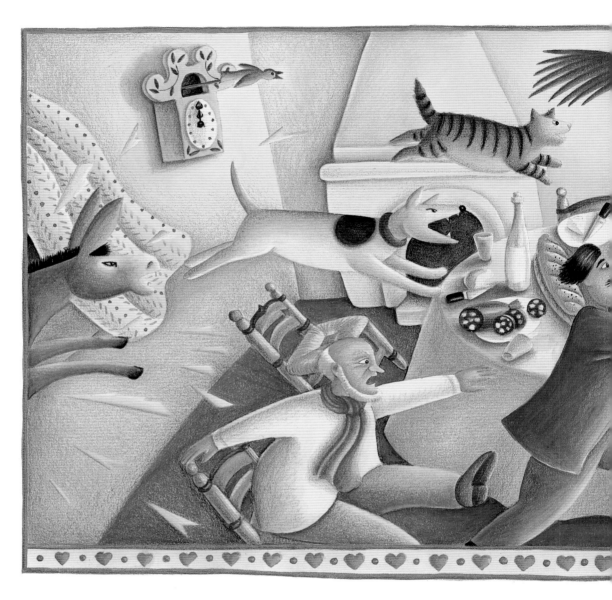

The old donkey brayed with all his strength, the old dog barked, the old cat meowed, and the old cock crowed. They made such a tremendous noise that the windowpanes splintered and crashed. The cock went flying into the cottage, after him jumped the cat, after the cat, the dog, and last of all, the old donkey went tumbling into the room.

The robbers were so frightened by the musicians' unearthly sounds, they jumped up thinking that a huge monster had burst in on them. They dropped everything, took to their heels, and were off as fast as they could be into the forest.

   45

The donkey and his friends sat at the table and ate and drank to their hearts' content. As soon as they had finished, they put out the light and each animal found a suitable sleeping place. The donkey stretched out on some straw, the dog lay behind the door, the cat curled up on the hearth near the warm ashes, and the cock perched on a beam that ran across the room. Exhausted by their long walk, they were soon fast asleep.

The robbers in the forest were not asleep at all. They were watching and waiting at a distance. When all was quiet and the light went out, they became braver. The chief robber sent one of his men to see what was happening in the cottage.

All was still and quiet as the robber slipped through the open window. He saw a pair of eyes shining by the hearth, and he thought they must be some glowing embers. He needed light, so he held a match to the glow, expecting the match to take fire. Instead the cat flew in his face, spitting, hissing, and scratching him all over. The robber was so afraid that he made for the door. The dog, sleeping on the mat by the door, woke up and bit the robber as hard as he could in the leg. As the robber limped over the straw where the donkey was stretched out, the donkey kicked him so hard with both hind legs that he flew right over to where the cock was perched. The cock screeched madly, "Cock-a-doodle-doo, cock-a-doodle-doo!"

The robber ran back to the forest as fast as he could, crying out, "We must get out of here. The cottage has been taken over by a huge monster with fingernails like those of a witch and huge teeth like those of a lion and hooves like those of the devil and a voice as terrible as the wind."

The robbers were so afraid that they all ran away as fast as they could, never to return to the house again.

As for the four friends, they stayed in the cottage, making the short journey every day along the road to Bremen, where they became very famous musicians.

If you are ever in Germany, you should go to the beautiful town of Bremen where you will see in front of the Town Hall a statue of a donkey and standing on his back a dog, and standing on his back a cat, and perched on her back a cock, in memory of the four old animals who ran away from death and journeyed along the road into the wide, wide world, looking for a new life, a new chance... and found it.

47

NEVER TRUST A PELICAN

THAI

Many, many miles away there is a land of great beauty, where the people dance and sing the animal stories they have heard told, over and over again, by the village storyteller.

Many moons ago there was in this land a very beautiful lake. It was surrounded by a deep, green forest and high mountains. A mighty river flowed into the lake, a river that came from a spring in the mountains, a river that journeyed far and wide over rocks and cascades, tumbling down waterfalls and winding its way until it reached the beautiful lake. The lake was full of life, full of plants, full of frogs and fish and even crabs.

Now, there was also a lone pelican living alongside the lake. This pelican had lost his family and friends long, long ago.

He was old and feeble and lived by the side of the lake all alone. Every day the pelican waded his way into the deeper water to catch the little, juicy fish that swam by. But now that he was getting older and weaker, he was finding it more and more difficult to catch the little, playful fish. Most days the pelican went home hungry and miserable. He realized that he would soon starve to death if he didn't catch a single fish.

One bright day the pelican was staring into the water wondering how he could make a plan to catch the fish without so much effort. Suddenly, upon seeing his own reflection in the water and recognizing what a wonderful and clever bird he was, a tremendous and most cunning idea came into his head.

"Yes!" he laughed out loud. "That's exactly what I will do!"

So the pelican put his plan into action.

The pelican stood by the side of the lake looking very sad
indeed. He wasn't even tempted to try and catch the fish
swimming past him. The creatures of the lake noticed how very
sad the pelican was and they began to wonder what had happened
to him.

The old crab, who was the wisest and most courageous of all
the creatures of the lake, came up to the pelican and asked,
"Why are you so sad, Pelican?"

"Oh dear, oh dear, oh dear me," replied the pelican. "There are
such bad times coming to this lake; such great danger is coming to
all of us animals."

"Dear me! Dear me! What is this great danger? Please tell me,"
said the crab.

"Indeed, we are all in very great danger," proclaimed the
pelican. "Soon no more water will flow down from the mountain.

The river will cease to tumble over the rocks, and the lake will dry up to nothing. We will all die and vanish."

The crab was most alarmed and passed on the news to the fish and frogs. The fish were even more alarmed. After all, the pelican could fly off and the frogs could hop off and the crabs could creep off sideways. But what about the fish? They could neither fly, hop, nor creep.

The poor fish panicked and swam around and around in circles, wailing, "What will become of us and our little babies? What will become of us?"

The largest and fattest of all the fish then came up to the pelican and said, "Dear Pelican, you have indeed given us very bad news. But you are a clever one. Please tell us how we can save ourselves."

The pelican replied, "I am only a bird, but I may be able to help you in a very small way." He continued, "There is another lake even larger and more beautiful a little distance from here. This lake has a never-ending spring in the center of it. The water there will never stop. The lake will never dry up. I can take you there if you wish."

"You are indeed a good friend," said the fish. "You can save us. Please take us in your beak to that other lake."

"It is an extremely difficult task," said the pelican. "But I will do my best."

When they heard this, all the fish began to cry out, "Take me first, take me first."

"Be patient," said the pelican. "I can only carry a few of you at a time. But I will make as many journeys as I need to. I am very old and feeble now and I may need to have lots of rests between journeys, so this task may take some time. But I do promise to save you all."

The pelican chose the plumpest of the fish, seized them in his beak, and flew off to the other side of the deep, green forest. He landed on a large rock and there in peace and quiet he ate them all up, leaving only a few fins and bones on the rock.

He then returned for more. He only had to say, "Who is next?"

"Me, me, take me," called the fish.

So he seized more fish and flew them to the rock, where he gobbled them up too.

Whenever the pelican was full, he rested and slept in the lovely, warm sun. Whenever the pelican was hungry, he flew back to the lake where more fish were eagerly awaiting their turn to be rescued.

Now, one day the oldest and wisest crab began to wonder about this great danger. He was very different from the fish, you see. He had traveled a great deal and had seen many things and had learned many things too. He began to realize that if the water was still flowing so strongly from the mountain, then the story of the drought was surely not true. In that case the pelican could not be trusted.

The oldest and wisest crab decided to find out what was going on. So the very next day when the pelican arrived at the lake and called out, "Who is next?" the crab said, "Take me, take me, dear Pelican."

The pelican was delighted. He was getting rather bored with so many fish. He suddenly developed a taste for crabmeat and readily agreed.

"I am at your service. Come, I will take you to the new lake."

The pelican seized the crab in his beak and flew over the deep, green forest to the large rock on the other side.

The wise, old crab looked down expecting to see a beautiful lake. But no, all he saw was a large rock covered with fins and bones. He knew at once what had happened.

The crab was afraid. He realized instantly that the pelican would land on the rock, kill him, and eat him up — just as he had done with all the fish. The crab thought and thought. What could he do to save himself and all the remaining fish in the lake?

All at once he seized the pelican around his neck with his strong pincers. The pelican struggled, flapped his wings in a panic, and tried his utmost to rid himself of the crab. But the crab held tight, pressing harder and harder on the bird's neck. Soon the pelican fell to the ground like a heavy stone, and that was the end of the pelican.

Slowly the crab made the long journey back to the lake, creeping sideways, as crabs usually do. When he finally reached the lake, the fish were very surprised to see him.

"Why have you come back? And where is the pelican?" they all cried. The old crab then told them how the pelican had been cheating them and how he had put an end to the pelican....

From that day to this, frogs, fish, and crabs have never made friends with pelicans.

THE MONKEY'S HEART

AFRICAN

A long time ago in Africa there lived an old tortoise who had a very strange and wonderful dream about a magical tree that grew all the fruits of the earth. She told her friends about her dream and together they set off in search of the tree's secret hiding place. Tortoise led, Lion followed, then came Hippopotamus, Giraffe, Elephant, Monkey, Zebra, Hyena, and Gazelle. They searched high and low, until one day they reached the secret place where the tree grew. It was the most beautiful sight the animals had ever seen, a tree with every fruit of the earth. Tortoise said the magic word to bring down the fruit and the animals ate as much as they could. Just as they were about to go home, Tortoise proclaimed, "Each one of us must

take a different

seed and plant it in the earth so

that fruit trees of every kind grow all over

the world."

And this was exactly what all the animals did.

Monkey took a mango seed and planted it in his favorite spot by the river. When the mango tree was fully grown, it produced the most delicious mangoes. Monkey made his home in that wonderful tree and enjoyed its juicy fruit.

Being a friendly and generous monkey, he shared his fruit with all the other animals in the jungle. Each day the mango tree would be surrounded by his friends: Lion, Hippopotamus, Zebra, Giraffe, Tortoise, and the others. They would chatter and joke away, enjoying the fruit at the same time.

One day a crocodile swam upriver and seeing the crowd of animals around the mango tree, he stopped a little way off to observe what was going on. Suddenly Monkey saw Crocodile, whom he had never met before. Monkey invited him to taste his lovely mangoes.

"Would you like a mango?" said Monkey.

"I've never had one before," replied Crocodile.

"Catch!" called Monkey.

Crocodile munched the mango and said, "That was very delicious. Thank you, Monkey."

And so Monkey threw down many, many more mangoes. Crocodile stayed on for a long chat. From that day on, Crocodile swam upriver to visit Monkey every day, and they became the best of friends.

One day as they were chatting about this and that, Crocodile mentioned that he lived with the Crocodile tribe and that their great chief was very important and very clever. Monkey said, "You should have told me about your chief before, so that I could send him a present of lovely, juicy mangoes."

Crocodile agreed that his chief would like to try the mangoes. So Monkey plucked plenty of mangoes and threw them into

Crocodile's open mouth. Crocodile swam back to his tribe with a mouthful of mangoes. He shared the mangoes with the chief and the other crocodiles in his tribe. He told them about his great new friend, Monkey.

The chief liked the mangoes very much. He asked Crocodile to bring more, and Crocodile promised to bring some mangoes home every time he visited Monkey.

After a while, a thought occurred to the chief. If Monkey eats such delicious mangoes every day, what a delicious dinner Monkey would make. If only he could get Monkey here. But knowing how fond of Monkey Crocodile was, it would be difficult to have Monkey for his dinner. So the chief thought of a brilliant plan.

As Crocodile returned from his outing, the chief lay himself down at the bottom of the river and pretended to be very ill. Crocodile swam up to the chief and asked, "What's the matter with you, my dear chief?"

The chief replied, "I am very ill and the Witch Doctor has told me that only the heart of a monkey can cure me. You must bring me a monkey's heart at once, otherwise I will surely die."

Crocodile was at a loss. Where could he find a monkey's heart? Monkeys were difficult to catch. Then suddenly he remembered his friend Monkey living in the mango tree. Very sadly he thought to himself, Oh dear, oh dear, what shall I do? I love that little monkey. He is my great friend. But I also love my chief. He is my great leader and he will die if he doesn't eat the heart of a monkey.

Poor Crocodile went around and around in circles trying to decide what to do, but in the end he thought that the chief was more important and that he would bring him Monkey's heart.

Early the next morning Crocodile set off to Monkey's home in the mango tree. All the way he was devising a plan. As usual, Monkey was delighted to see his friend.

"Hello there, my friend. I'm happy to see you this morning."

Crocodile had made a good plan to catch Monkey and said, "Monkey, you have been very kind to me these past few weeks, giving me and my tribe such wonderful fruit. I should like to do something for you in return." Crocodile continued, "For a long time I have wanted to invite you to my home across the river to meet my tribe and offer you hospitality. My chief would be very honored to make your acquaintance."

Monkey replied, "How sweet of you to invite me to your home. I too would like to meet your chief and your tribe, but how can I get there? You live in the water. I would drown if I tried to go to your place. You see, dear Crocodile, I can't swim."

"That's easily settled," replied Crocodile. "We live on the riverbank as well as in the river. I can take you there. Sit on my back and I'll ferry you across."

Monkey agreed. He was happy that he had such a good friend as Crocodile. Monkey jumped down from the mango tree and landed on Crocodile's back. Crocodile swam across the river with Monkey sitting on his back. On reaching the middle of the river, Crocodile began to sink lower and lower into the water. He thought that it would be a good idea to drown Monkey before they got to his riverbank. Down, down they went, deeper into the water. Monkey called out, "I'm getting wet, Crocodile, please don't go down."

There was silence as Crocodile continued to go down, down, deeper into the water. At once Monkey realized that something was wrong. He was very frightened. He cried out, "What are you doing? I will drown if you go down any farther." Crocodile replied, "I cannot hide the truth from you, my dear friend. My chief is very ill and will die if he doesn't eat a monkey's heart."

Monkey was shocked and terrified. He bit his lip to stop himself from crying while he thought of a plan to save himself. At last he said as calmly as he could, "My friend, why didn't you tell me before that you needed my heart to save your chief. I would have brought it with me."

"What! You don't have your heart with you?" asked Crocodile in surprise. "No!" said Monkey. "I always leave my heart in the mango tree when I go on a journey. Let's go back at once and get my heart for your chief."

Crocodile turned around and quickly swam back to the mango tree. When they got there, Monkey jumped off Crocodile's back and hurried up the tree calling, "You stupid crocodile. Didn't you know that monkeys keep their hearts in their breast, like everyone else. You foolish old crocodile. Did you really expect me to come back with you to your tribe to be killed?"

Monkey laughed and laughed.

"Go back to your tribe. Our friendship is ended."

Crocodile swam back down the river feeling very ashamed. He shed a big crocodile tear as he realized how foolish he had been and that now he had lost his best friend.

Monkey laughed and laughed and threw rotten mangoes after the silly old crocodile.

All the animals in the jungle heard Monkey laugh so loud that they came to see what it was about. They surrounded the

mango tree and listened to Monkey telling them how he had outwitted Crocodile, warning them never to make friends with a crocodile if they wanted to reach a good old age like Tortoise.

SEDNA AND KING GULL

CANADIAN / INUIT

In a very cold place, where the land is ice and snow, rocks and mountains; where the sea is forever raging and the winds howling; where the winters are long and dark; in this cold, harsh place live the Inuit people.

The Inuits tell many stories from a time when unbelievable things could happen. In those days fabulous spirits and magical creatures inhabited the frozen lands.... Maybe they still do, who knows?

Sedna lived in this cold land. Sedna was a very beautiful girl with long, dark hair and large, dark eyes as black as the midnight sky. She lived in an igloo between the wild clouds and the freezing icebergs. She lived with her father —

a brave, old hunter who devoted his life to bringing up his beloved daughter.

Sedna and her father both spent the long, dark winter hunting, cooking, drying animal skins, and sewing clothes out of fur. In the spring the sun made the icebergs sparkle and brought a little warmth and hope to the tribe. As some of the snow melted, flowers appeared, covering the ground with a rich carpet of blue and yellow, purple and white.

During these sparkling days Sedna would run and play outside, not with other children but with the wild, free birds. She would dance to their flight and sing to their calling. Her very best friend was the king of the seagulls. He was very strong and beautiful, proud and powerful. He had huge wings and was covered with silver-gray feathers. His eyes shone like the stars in the sky. King Gull was greatly respected and deeply loved by the other birds in the kingdom.

There came a time when Sedna's father expected her to get married. Many young hunters came to court her. But Sedna was not interested in any of them.

Her father became worried. He would say, "Sedna, I will not always be alive to hunt for you. It is time you chose a nice, young hunter who can take care of you. You must stop dreaming and dancing with the birds, they are not your kind."

But Sedna would toss her raven-black hair and answer back, "Dear Father, there is not a man in the world that I want to marry."

You see, in her heart Sedna loved the king gull and wanted to marry him. But she was afraid of upsetting her father, and this made her sad. At the very moment Sedna was thinking these thoughts, the king gull flew overhead and saw her sadness. He felt a great warmth in his heart and also knew that he wanted to marry Sedna.

Using his magical powers, he turned himself into a man. Thus disguised, he came to the igloo and asked for Sedna's hand in marriage. Sedna was delighted. She could hardly contain her happiness when she recognized who this young man really was. Her father agreed to the match. And so it was that Sedna and the king gull were to leave her homeland and go to live in the place of the birds. Sedna kissed her father good-bye. He wished her good luck as he let her go forever.

She came to the seafront where a kayak was waiting for her. She sat in the kayak and away they paddled to the far-off land of the birds. When at last they reached King Gull's kingdom, he led Sedna to his ice cave, which he had prepared for her, lining it with soft, white feathers. He had also made her a thick blanket of feathers as fine as silk so that she would always keep warm. Sedna

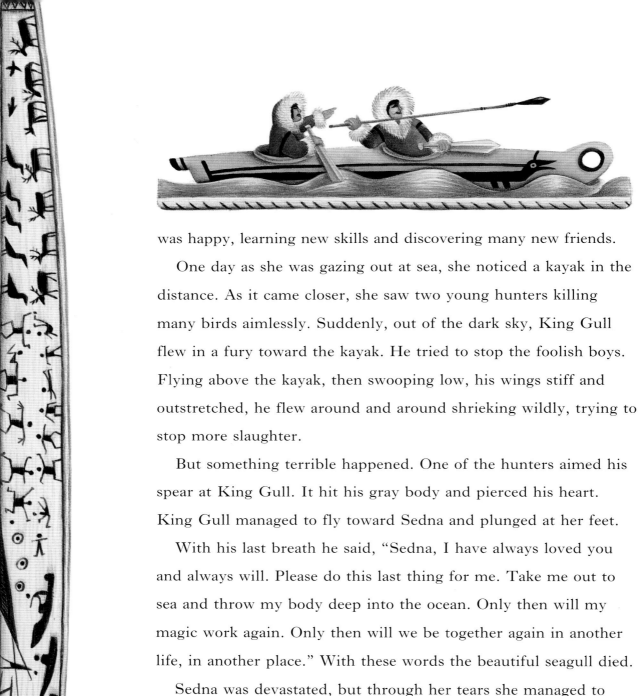

was happy, learning new skills and discovering many new friends.

One day as she was gazing out at sea, she noticed a kayak in the distance. As it came closer, she saw two young hunters killing many birds aimlessly. Suddenly, out of the dark sky, King Gull flew in a fury toward the kayak. He tried to stop the foolish boys. Flying above the kayak, then swooping low, his wings stiff and outstretched, he flew around and around shrieking wildly, trying to stop more slaughter.

But something terrible happened. One of the hunters aimed his spear at King Gull. It hit his gray body and pierced his heart. King Gull managed to fly toward Sedna and plunged at her feet.

With his last breath he said, "Sedna, I have always loved you and always will. Please do this last thing for me. Take me out to sea and throw my body deep into the ocean. Only then will my magic work again. Only then will we be together again in another life, in another place." With these words the beautiful seagull died.

Sedna was devastated, but through her tears she managed to find a kayak and gently placed her beloved bird inside. She paddled far out to sea. When they were far away, she stopped and picked up her dear friend. She kissed King Gull and threw him

68

into the icy water. At that very moment the sky darkened. There
was a flash of lightning and a clap of thunder. When Sedna
looked up again the sky was full of birds. Thousands and
thousands of birds of every size and kind flew around and around,
up and down, screeching and singing, "King Gull is dead! King
Gull is dead!"

Others were calling, "Sea creatures are born! Sea creatures are
born!" Sedna was very moved by this sight. Still crying, she
leaned over the side of the kayak and looked deep into the sea.
There she saw, to her amazement, the king gull transforming
magically into a huge whale.

In this time of magic, as her tears were falling into the water,
they were transformed into walruses, seals, dolphins, octopuses,
sea horses, and fish and creatures of every kind.

In this moment of magic the sea creatures came to be. They all surrounded the kayak as if to say, "Join us, Sedna, be our queen." Sedna dove into the icy water and she did indeed become the sea queen, the sea spirit, Mother of the Sea. It was now Sedna's task to take care of all the sea creatures of the world.

Because of the hunters' cruelty in killing aimlessly, Sedna made a sea law. Hunters were only permitted to hunt for food and skins,

and only as much as they needed for their tribe to survive and no
more. If this law was ever broken, Sedna would call up fierce
storms, the sea would swell and rage, thus preventing men from
hunting. Then only if the shaman of the tribe dove into the sea
and swam down to visit Sedna under the water, giving her news of
the Inuit people, only then would she calm the sea again so that
hunting could resume.

MAGIC IN THE RAIN FOREST

BRAZILIAN

There was a time in the old days when there was no darkness, no night, no sleep. In that time there was only light, only day, only waking. But the great old trees that lived in the rain forest knew many things. It was their wisdom that first brought night out of the river into the world.

The old trees cast their magic far and wide across the rain forest. As they did so, all living creatures were born. The sticks and the roots in the forest turned into animals. The leaves on the trees turned into birds. The stones and pebbles in the rivers turned into fish and snails. The toucan, the quetzal, the humming-bird, and the parrot were made. The armadillo, the anteater, the tapir, and the jaguar were made. The coral snake, the piranha, and the turtle were made. It all happened in that very moment when the old trees brought night to the earth.

In the darkness Snake slithered along the riverbank looking at his beautiful eyes reflected in the water. As he did so, he sang:

"Eyes, eyes, twinkling bright

Dance for me

In the magic of the night."

And his eyes popped out of his head and danced on the surface of the water.

At that very moment Jaguar was walking along the riverbank looking at his beautiful body reflected in the water. All of a sudden he noticed Snake's eyes dancing on the surface of the water.

He lay down in the long grass perfectly still, perfectly silent, and watched. After a while Snake sang,

"Eyes, eyes, twinkling bright

Dance back to me

In the magic of the night."

And his eyes danced back across the surface of the water straight into his head.

Jaguar was amazed by what he had just seen. He went up to Snake and asked, "How can you do this wonderful thing?"

Snake, rather pleased at the chance of showing off, repeated his song. Again, his eyes popped out of his head, and like fireflies they danced all over the river in the moonlight. After a while

Snake sang once more and his eyes danced back to him.

Jaguar was even more amazed. He said, "I would like my eyes to dance like that. Please teach me the trick." Snake agreed but warned, "This is no trick. This is magic and magic can be dangerous!" But Jaguar didn't care. He just wanted his eyes to dance on the water. So Snake began to sing,

> "Jaguar's eyes, twinkling bright
>
> Dance for him
>
> In the magic of the night."

And sure enough, Jaguar's eyes popped out of his head and danced across the river. After a while Snake sang,

"Jaguar's eyes, twinkling bright

Dance back to him

In the magic of the night."

Jaguar was so thrilled, he wanted another turn. "That was wonderful. Do it again."

"No, it's not safe," replied Snake.

"Please, please, do it again. Just once more," pleaded Jaguar.

Snake gave in. But this time as Jaguar's eyes were dancing on the water, he sang,

"Jaguar's eyes, twinkling bright

Dance back to ME

In the magic of the night."

And as Jaguar's eyes came dancing toward Snake, his tongue flicked out and swallowed the eyes. He turned and slithered away into the forest, into the night. Poor Jaguar couldn't see anything; frightened and lonely, he wandered through the forest, not knowing where he was going, not knowing what he was to do. Unable to hunt without his eyes, he was doomed to starve to death. In his despair, he lay down under a wise old tree. He put his paws over his empty eye sockets and moaned softly.

The tree felt very sorry for Jaguar. He decided to help the sad animal. Using his magical powers, he called for his friend Harpy Eagle.

Harpy Eagle came flying by and hovered just above Jaguar. "Why are you so sad?" she asked. Jaguar told her the strange story. The bird said, "Yes, these are indeed strange times. In the darkness of the night, many mysterious things can happen. Wait here, and I will see what I can do to help." With these words, Harpy Eagle flew over the forest and far away, looking, listening until her keen eyes spied Snake slithering toward a lake. Harpy Eagle flew up to Snake. Hovering above him, she said, "I have heard that you can make your eyes dance over the water."

"Yes," replied Snake, "that's true."

Harpy Eagle said, "I find it very hard to believe. It is surely not possible."

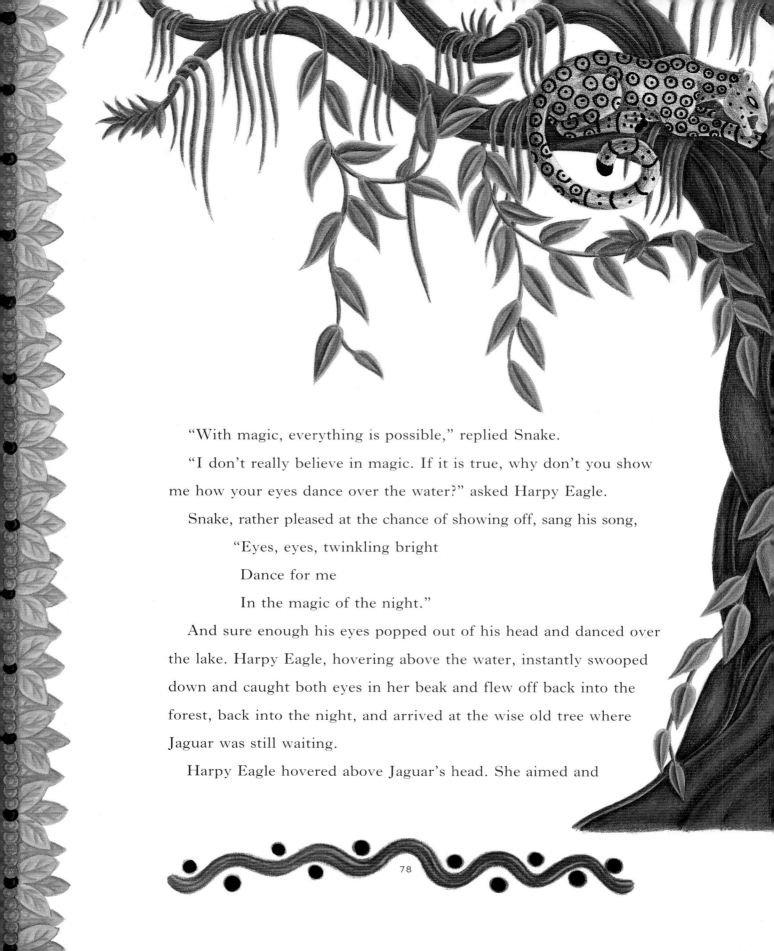

"With magic, everything is possible," replied Snake.

"I don't really believe in magic. If it is true, why don't you show me how your eyes dance over the water?" asked Harpy Eagle.

Snake, rather pleased at the chance of showing off, sang his song,

> "Eyes, eyes, twinkling bright
>
> Dance for me
>
> In the magic of the night."

And sure enough his eyes popped out of his head and danced over the lake. Harpy Eagle, hovering above the water, instantly swooped down and caught both eyes in her beak and flew off back into the forest, back into the night, and arrived at the wise old tree where Jaguar was still waiting.

Harpy Eagle hovered above Jaguar's head. She aimed and

dropped both eyes perfectly into the sockets in Jaguar's head.

Jaguar could see again. In fact, he could see better and farther than before. He looked at his reflection in the river. He was astonished at how beautiful and bright his new eyes were.

"Thank you, my friend. How can I repay you?" he said.

"I am very hungry. Why don't you hunt me a tapir, my favorite meat?" replied Harpy Eagle.

So Jaguar caught a large tapir, and the two new friends enjoyed a delicious feast.

Ever since that night Jaguar has always left part of his kill for Harpy Eagle in gratitude for his sparkling new eyes. And as for Snake's eyes, they grew back again, staring, glaring, shining bright, but never again to dance in the magic of the night.

ABOUT THE STORIES

I am a storyteller. I travel from community to community, from school to school, from theater to theater, and from country to country telling the stories I have collected throughout my life.

These experiences often bring me in contact with other storytellers, and we share our favorite tales, widening the range of their appeal. While written versions exist for many of the tales in this collection, and a few of my retellings are inspired by sources indicated below, more often it is a particular storyteller whom I have to thank here. –N.A.

GRANDMOTHER SPIDER

NATIVE AMERICAN

I first read this Cherokee story in *Storymaking in Education and Therapy*, published by Jessica Kingsley Publishers, and then adapted it for a young audience.

THE RABBIT IN THE MOON

INDIAN

A Buddhist monk named Dayatmananda told me this story at the Ramakrishna Vedanta Centre in Buckinghamshire, England.

THE DRAGON AND THE COCKEREL

CHINESE

I heard this story during a workshop I ran on shadow puppets at the Chinese Community Centre, Soho, London. Weng Naigiang, one of the participants, used it to create a delightful shadow play.

THE GREEDY FROG

AUSTRALIAN

Wendy Watson, an Aborigine storyteller, told me stories of her people, including this one, at an exhibition of Aboriginal paintings at the Hayward Gallery in London.

THE MUSICIANS OF BREMEN

GERMAN

While numerous retellings of this popular Grimm story exist, my version was inspired by my grandfather.

NEVER TRUST A PELICAN

THAI

I first encountered this story as a mime show by an Asian mime and dance company at Tara Arts Centre in southwest London. I then adapted it to be told with words and movement.

THE MONKEY'S HEART

AFRICAN

I heard Kofi Oswaggo, a marvelous storyteller from Kenya, tell this story, among others, at an "African village" festival held in Kew Gardens, London. He explained that the stories are tribal, meaning that each tribe has its own version stemming from a common storyline. The story in this collection is Kenyan but is found in other versions in Tanzania and Ghana.

SEDNA AND KING GULL

CANADIAN

Two Inuit throat singers told me this story at a storytelling festival at Queen Elizabeth Hall in London. They were both very tiny women who made extraordinary sounds with their throats, sounding somewhat like whales and dolphins, seals and seagulls.

MAGIC IN THE RAIN FOREST

BRAZILIAN

I met Inti Ramos, a Brazilian Indian, when I was telling stories at the Museum of Mankind in London. We then spent a few days walking in the Welsh hills and exchanging stories from our different cultures. Inti told me this one.